<u>Storywriter</u>
Arriane Mae Bolasco Munar, Psy.D.

CAN WE TALK?

A SHORT STORY OF NAVIGATING IDENTITY AND BELONGING AS TEENS OF IMMIGRANT PARENTS

<u>AUTHOR</u>
JACKIE VIERNES, M.A.

<u>ILLUSTRATOR</u>
ALLYN CRUZ

This book, and my clinical dissertation from
which it was conceived, is a love letter to my mom.
May this book be the catalyst for healing
other parent-child relationships in time.

Contents

PART ONE

TOGETHER

"Mom, I already told you I'm not going to go to the online workshop. It's **_SUMMER_**!"

"Mark! Ay my God, just GO. You're already just on the computer all day. Angeli will also go, too!"

"*Huuuuh?* Mom, it's too soon for me! I don't need to go to that yet."

"*Ay Dios ko*[1], Angeli. Go so that your brother will also go, okay?"

---

[1] *(Tagalog)* "Oh my God!"

The De Los Santos family were tensely making their way towards the town's Fourth of July event at the local high school. As they approached, the red letters for *College Application Online Workshop* flashed on the LED sign. This is the summer before Mark's senior year and his mom kept urging him to use this summer to research colleges and how to apply. But Mark wasn't interested at all. He didn't know what he wanted to do, nor did he know what college to even look at.

"Actually," Mark interjected, "I was thinking about going to community college first, Ma," Mark spoke with a small voice that caused an eruption from his mom.

Mark's mom exclaimed, "Community college?! No way. You will never get into medical school or law school with community college!"

Mark's mom proceeded to yell at Mark as the family came to a parking spot near the football field. As his mom rang on, Mark slowly became more and more defeated with standing up for himself. Law school? Medical school? When did Mark ever say that he wanted to be a lawyer or a doctor? Right as the car was put in park, Mark burst out of the car and started walking towards campus, suddenly feeling the pressure from the line of lawyers and doctors in his Filipino[2] family.

"Ay my goodness, MARK!", his mom shouted. "Where

____

[2] **Filipino:** Hailing from the Philippines, a country in the southeast region of Asia

are you going?! Get back here! Ay naku[3], Angeli, you go with your brother! I don't know why he's being like that."

Angeli, Mark's little sister, was annoyed with their constant bickering and started fidgeting with her hijab[4]. She felt as though every time they fought, she was always the one who had to get Mark to agree with their mom, even if she didn't agree with her herself.

"Ma, why do I need to go after him? He's fine! He's probably going to meet up with Sai," she points to a small girl with beautiful, dark skin in the direction that Mark was headed toward. "Why can't I just stay here with you and Pa?" Angeli did little stomps of frustration because she was sick of following Mark around like the babysitter of a child. He was 17 and Angeli was only 14, how was she supposed to take care of him?

"Do not argue, Angeli. You go with your brother. Remember when you didn't watch him? Do you want that to happen again?!" She pointed aggressively at Mark as he started to walk up to Sai, further into the crowd. "Mark, you better behave!" She yelled across the parking lot.

"Fine, I'll go." Angeli always felt helpless whenever their mom brought up the incident that happened with Mark before summer started. Even so, Mark didn't need a babysitter, but their mom felt like he was always up to no good. Angeli sulkily walked

---

[3] *(Tagalog)* *"Oh my."*

[4] **Hijab:** A head covering worn in public by some Muslim women.

toward Mark, who was making his way to Sai.

Sai Singh, an Indian[5] girl entering her senior year of high school, was in deep thought while looking down at her feet when she heard her name being called.

"Sai! Wait up!" Mark ran to her with an angry expression on his face.

"It looks like Mark and his mom fought again," Sai thought. She grabbed her phone and opened the front camera to check her face. Her eyes were still red and puffy from crying earlier. She hoped that Mark wouldn't notice, but then again, he always noticed.

Mark caught up to Sai and noted her glossy eyes. Seeing his friend in distress made Mark forget about his own drama, "Hey, Sai, are you okay?" He lightly touched her shoulder in sympathy. As Mark comforted her, Angeli caught up to them and, noticing Sai's fragile state, also rested her hand on Sai's shoulder.

Sai took a deep breath and looked back down at her feet while twiddling her fingers.

"It's just that…" she paused as her voice trembled, "I've been hiding my report card and my mom found it in my room. My parents are so… disappointed in me. They didn't even want to drop me off here. It's like they're embarrassed to even be seen with me," Sai burst into tears and buried her face in her hands as Mark hugged her and Angeli patted her back.

---

[5] **Indian:** Hailing from India, a country in South Asia

Sai and the De Los Santos siblings were close because they shared issues with their parents around grades and expectations. But, even then, feeling understood by one another didn't make them feel any better about their relationship with their parents.

Unbeknownst to the trio, Benji Liang, a boy in Mark's class, and Lillian Vasquez, an incoming freshman, were walking in their direction.

"So, we were at my uncle's house, right?" Benji loudly says to Lillian, enough for the others to overhear. "And then my parents start telling me how great my cousins are at school, sports, all that type of stuff and they want me to do the same here. But it's like, why can't they see I'm already doing a lot? Like, *I* directed the school's play in April *and* I've been in the marching band since freshman year! And they're still like, 'Oh, why can't you be more like your Hong Kong[6] cousins?!' I'm so tired of it!"

Lillian listened empathetically to Benji while patting his shoulder. She understood Benji even though they had only met this summer taking a Spanish class at the community college to fulfill their foreign language credit. Lillian had left her mother and her six younger siblings because of the same reason; not feeling good enough. Lillian worked hard, even voluntarily taking summer classes so that she could graduate high school early. However, all her Puerto Rican[7] mom could see was that her American daughter did not know their

---

[6] **Hong Kong:** A region on the southeastern coast of China.

[7] **Puerto Rican:** Hailing from Puerto Rico, an island in the Caribbean that is noted as a United States "territory".

home language well enough. Lillian didn't really know what she meant by that, especially since she was always the one translating for her mother.

Sai, excited to see her friend, interjected, "Hey Benji! This is Angeli and you probably know Mark already?" They greeted each other solemnly, noticing the tense air around each of them

"Hey, y'all. I've seen you two around campus, actually! This is Lillian. She's an incoming freshman but we both met over the summer in Spanish class at the community college!"

"Hi," Lillian shyly whispered.

"Whoa, community college classes already?! You're barely a freshman!" Mark exclaimed.

Lillian replied, "I'm trying to graduate early. The sooner I graduate, the sooner I can leave for college." Benji gives Lillian a reassuring squeeze on her shoulder. "Yeah, we just didn't want to be around our families right now. It's way too much. How about y'all? Why aren't you setting up for the fireworks?"

"Honestly, Benji," Angeli says, "we're feeling the same."

.The group looked at one another with a silent understanding they were not aware of earlier. It dawned on them that they were all collectively going through some drama with their parents and that being with each other, even though some of them weren't close, was better than being with their families right now.

Mark, still wanting to get as far away from his mom, who was now waving her hands at him to come back, realized he could take them to the place where the incident happened. The incident that made his mom never trust him again.

"Come on, I know a place."

As Mark leads the group through the campus and out of the crowd, Angeli spots Flo around the corner of the student bathrooms.

"FLO! Over here!" Angeli yells.

Flo Bautista, sitting on the bike racks, was with Shiloh and Frankie. From a distance, it looked like Shiloh was talking passionately about something upsetting, but the group couldn't make out what was being said. Flo, hearing Angeli, looked up and saw her waving at her to come over. Flo started to make her way over with Shiloh, who was assisting Frankie by pushing his wheelchair to follow Flo.

"FLO! What the heck! Why haven't you been texting me back?!" Angeli gave Flo a soft shove.

"Dude, it wasn't my fault! My parents took my phone away and said I won't get it until school starts." Flo rolled her eyes, "They think that I might go out and do drugs or something? Which I've never even done, by the way. But now they're keeping a close eye on me. This has been the first time I've been out all summer!" Flo raises her arms in frustration over her parents' strict rules over baseless accusations.

After seeing terrifying news reports from Guatemala[8] and local news about the rise of teens using drugs that have gotten in trouble with the law, seriously injured, or worse, Flo's parents became paranoid that she would go to parties and do dangerous things, too.

After some begging and compromising, they finally allowed her out for the Fourth of July. Since they knew several faculty members from the school would be there, they figured that Flo wouldn't try anything sneaky because someone would surely see her and report it back to them.

Among the trio, the group was surprised to see Shiloh Santiago, a Oaxacan[9] student who had never gone to any events for the high school, let alone the community.

"Shiloh? Hey! How are you?" Mark excitedly asks. He then turns to Sai and says, "Doesn't he seem different, Sai? His hair is longer, his voice is different, his-"

"It's 'they.'" Shiloh interjected with their correct pronouns.

Mark, feeling embarrassed, gave a quiet, "Sorry," and stuffed his hands into his pockets. Mark awkwardly asks, "So, what were you guys talking about?"

---

[8] **Guatemala**: A Central American country.

[9] **Oaxacan**: Hailing from Oaxaca (*wuh-HAH-kah*), a state within Mexico known for its preservation of indigenous cultures.

Frankie started, "Shiloh was just saying-" when Shiloh nudged at Frankie's chair and shot him a stern look.

He continued, "Um... Nothing." To interrupt the awkward silence, he quickly adds, "Soooooooooo, where were y'all headed?"

Mark replies, hands still in his pockets, "Oh, we were going up to this spot I know, Y'all should come! We all needed a break from our parents so we're getting away for a while." Mark rounded his back and began to sneakily lead the group. Frankie, Shiloh, and Flo looked at each other and nonchalantly followed Mark.

As they made their way, Mark led them further away from the football field to the back of the school. The back of the school was lined with a row of trees that had a small opening, which was easy to miss if one wasn't looking for it. Stopping at the entrance, Mark turns to the group and puts his index finger to his lips, making a *shhhh* sound. As the group made their way to the opening, they were greeted by a grassy incline that led to the top of a hill. The group steadily climbed in silence, eager to see the view beyond the clearing. The only sound that can be heard is the soft summer wind blowing through the hill's grass.

Suddenly, as they made their way close to the top, the sound of crying became louder and louder. Beyond the clearing, the group saw Jaya, one of Benji and Mark's classmates, comforting Ricardo De León, who was crying next to her.

"Jaya? How do you know this spot?" Benji huffed in exhaustion from the steep climb.

"Oh, Mark took me here one time! I was going
through some things and he showed me this place.
You don't mind, right, Mark? My friend Ricardo is
dealing with some problems with his dad, and he
needed to breathe." Ricardo feels Jaya's voice
vibrating from talking and looks up to see the group
standing above him. Jaya signs, "These are some of
my friends" to Ricardo as he picks up his cochlear
implant, decorated with the Mexican[10] flag, and
reattaches it to his ear while wiping his eyes.

"Not at all. This spot is for everyone." Mark raised his
arm and showcased the hill that they were now on. It
was a secluded hill that was high enough to where the
festivities below were heard as a faint echo. It was
grassy with a small trail that led to the edge of the hill.
The other side overlooked a small part of their town;
small lights of cars, streetlights, and houses twinkling
along the horizon.

"Are you okay?" Lillian asks Ricardo, who is angrily
crying in Jaya's arms.

Ricardo looks up, jumps to his feet, and yells, "My dad
is so unfair! It's the same thing every time, and it's not
my fault! I cry at *everything*, okay? I'll cry at a stray
dog, when people sing me *Happy Birthday*... Heck! I
even cried when I saw Jaya today! Every single time,
my dad tells me to stop being emotional and that 'boys
don't cry' and blah blah blah. When I saw Jaya earlier
and started to tear up, my dad straight up *LEAVES*.
He left me here *alone*! Then I get this text, right?"
Ricardo grabs his phone from his pocket and opens

---

[10] **Mexican**: Hailing from Mexico, a country on the southern border of
the United States.

his dad's text that reads, "I left. Come home when you're done crying and you're ready to be a real man."

The group read the text and understood Ricardo's crying even more. Ricardo puts his face in his hands, sits on the grass, and cries even harder after re-reading the text, as if opening up a wound that was not finished healing. Jaya follows suit and puts her arm around Ricardo's shoulders, touching her head against his in comfort. Slowly, each member of the group sat down together in a circle, wanting to enclose Ricardo in a safe space where he felt okay to cry as much as he wanted.

Part Two

Release

The silence that permeated the group was sprinkled with periodic sniffles from Ricardo, who was beginning to calm down. He noticed Lillian, whom he remembers from middle school. "Oh, Lillian," he wipes the last of his tears with his sweater, "I'm sorry you have to see me like this. What are you doing here? I saw your mom and siblings earlier, so I thought you'd be with them?"

Lillian shifts her sitting position, so her knees are now to her chest. As she hugs her knees, she rests her chin on her arms, "Yeah," she paused, "I was with them, but I just... needed to get away."

13

Before Lillian was with Benji, she was with her family, which consisted of her single mother and her six younger siblings. She was the oldest of the bunch so, naturally, her mom relied on her to help take care of her siblings.

"Lillita, ¡vela los nenes por favor! Que estoy intentando hacer algo."[11] Lillian's mom motioned to Lillian's siblings with a wave of her hand. Lillian, who was texting Benji about his parents, didn't hear her mom. At the same time, the four youngest siblings were running circles around Lillian and the other two were tugging on her arms trying to get her attention.

"LILLIAN VASQUEZ!" Her mom yelled.

"Huh, what?" Lillian responded, "Ay perdón mama, es que no te escuche. Estaba texteando con mi compañero de la clase de Español extra que estoy cogiendo en community college. El esta aquí so puede que me encuentre con él y comamos piraguas."[12]

"¡No muchacha! ¿Y quien va a cuidar los nenes?"[13] Her mom asked while setting down the picnic blankets for the family to sit on.

Then, Lillian's teacher from middle school walked by the family and spotted her, "Oh, Lillian! Hi! It's so nice to see you." Mr. Johnson was Lillian's Algebra

---

[11] *(Spanish)* *"Watch the kids, please! I'm trying to do something."*

[12] *(Spanish)* *"Oh sorry, I didn't hear you. I was texting my friend from the extra Spanish class I take at the community college. He's here, so I might go meet up with him and get some shaved ice."*

[13] *(Spanish)* *"No, girl, who's going to take care of the kids?"*

teacher and was also one of her favorite teachers in her last year of middle school.

"Hey, Mr. Johnson," Lillian gave him a hug, "Mama, este era mi maestro de matemáticas."[14]

"Nice to meet you, Ms. Vasquez!" He extended his hand with a warm smile.

As Lillian's mom shook his hand, she smiled and offered a polite, "Hello," her Puerto Rican accent detectable.

"Your daughter is very bright. You must be so proud! I loved having her in my class and am very confident she's going to do so well in high school." Mr. Johnson smiled at the Vasquez family and waited for a reply. Lillian's mom looked to her daughter to translate what Mr. Johnson said.

"El dice que soy muy inteligente y que voy hacer muy bien en high school y que debes de estar muy orgullosa de mi,"[15] Lillian smiled at her mom, hoping that she would recognize how hard she works in school.

Her mom responded, "Muchas gracias por cuidar nuestra hija."

Mr. Johnson smiled at Lillian expectedly, who translated, "She's appreciative of you..." Lillian paused

---

14 (Spanish) "Mom, this was my math teacher."

15 (Spanish) "He says I'm very smart, that I'm going to do very good in high school, and that you should be proud of me."

for a few seconds to look for the right words before she continued, "For looking after me." Lillian picked up her 4-year-old sister who was tugging at the side of her shirt harshly.

"Oh, Lillian, please tell her that you are very independent for your age and all your brilliance is from you! I just teach math." Mr. Johnson laughed.

Lillian translated this back to her mom, who didn't understand why her daughter was considered independent; she's only 14 after all. She just smiled politely at Mr. Johnson without really acknowledging the compliment he gave to Lillian.

Lillian's other siblings were still running in circles around her. Mr. Johnson, seeing Lillian getting more and more occupied by her duties to her family, bid a farewell and a "Happy Fourth!" to the Vasquez family. Mr. Johnson noticed that Lillian looked very tired and didn't question it. Instead, he patted her shoulder and told her, "Stay in touch, okay, Lillian?" Lillian smiled at him, grateful that Mr. Johnson offered a small gesture of kindness in such a stressful situation.

Lillian put her sister down, but her sister anxiously reached her arms up to be carried again. Her siblings, who were running in circles around her, had finally stopped but were now whining, "I'm hungry! I'm hungry!" to Lillian.

"Lillian, saca la comida que metimos en la neveríta y asegúrate que los nenes coman. Hay unos cuantos sandwiches ahí."[16] Her mom started to unfold her camping chair so she could relax before the fireworks started.

Lillian sighed, took the sandwiches out of the cooler, and passed them to her siblings. Her youngest brother started complaining, "I don't *WANT* sandwiches! I want a hot dog! Lilli, can I get a hot dog instead?"

"Yeah! Hot dogs!" shouted one sibling

"Ooo, yeah, a hot dog sounds better!" yelled another sibling.

Lillian looked to her mother for help, but she was sitting on her camping chair, reading over a stack of papers titled *Rental Agreement* that she pulled out of her purse.

"Oye Lillian, cuando lleguemos a casa necesito que me ayudes con los papeles del acuerdo de renta. Yo no pude entenderlos muy bien."[17]

"Hot dog! Hot dog! Hot dog!" All six siblings started chanting to Lillian.

Lillian looked back and forth between her siblings and her mom, getting overwhelmed more and more by her siblings demanding hot dogs and her mother being

---

[16] *(Spanish)* "Lillian, get out the food that we put in the cooler and make sure that the kids eat. There are some sandwiches in there."

[17] *(Spanish)* "Hey Lillian, when we get home, I need you to help me with the rental agreement paperwork. I could not understand them very well."

too busy to help her.

"NO!" Lillian yelled. She had never yelled at her family before, shocked at the sound of her own voice.

Her siblings stopped chanting and her mother looked at her with bewilderment.

"¡Qué me dijiste!"[18] Her mom asked, standing up slowly in disbelief.

"I-, I-," Lillian choked, not wanting to cry in front of her family, "Voy a ir a ver a mi amiga por ahí."[19]

Lillian started to walk quickly away from her family, ignoring their pleas for her to come back to the blanket. She heard her siblings start chanting about hot dogs again while her mom tried desperately to get them to eat the sandwiches instead.

She blinked hard to stop herself from crying, bringing herself back to the present moment. As Lillian finished her story, she looked up to see the group listening empathetically.

"Wow, Lillian. You have so many responsibilities, always taking care of your siblings." Angeli could heavily relate to Lillian. She looked at Mark, thinking about her own responsibilities in "watching" him.

"Yeah," Frankie agreed, "Honestly, that's a lot. I have a lot of siblings too, but my parents mostly take care

---

[18] *(Spanish)* "What did you say?"

[19] *(Spanish)* "I'm going to go see my friend over there."

of them. I mean, I'll have to babysit here and there, but it sounds like you're their second mom!"

Lillian nodded, realizing that she never really felt like a typical teenager.

"I guess it's because I was born here, you know? English is my second language, just like her, but I definitely know it better than my mom does. I have to help her with a lot of adult stuff and take care of my siblings like I'm their second mom. Honestly, I don't mind when I do these things here and there, especially since she's a hard-working, single mom. But lately, it's been a lot. I just wanted to hang out with Benji here."

Lillian looked at Benji with a slight smile. They became really close after taking Spanish together at the local community college, especially since they were the only high school students in the class. She added, "I just wish she understood that I'm never going to be this young ever again, and I don't want to grow up too fast. I want to enjoy my youth."

"Do you think she knows you feel like that, Lillian?" Jaya asks.

"Oh," Lillian perks up, "Honestly, no. I don't think I'd ever tell her. She already does a lot for me and, even though it's overwhelming, it's the least I can do for her. She came here from Puerto Rico so we could all have a better life."

"That makes sense," Jaya empathized. "But it's also important that you take a break, too. If it becomes overwhelming to the point where you don't feel like a kid anymore, I think it's okay to ask for a break once in a while." Jaya put her hand on Lillian's shoulder for comfort.

As Lillian's shoulders relaxed under her touch, she finally felt the slightest hint of rest. She had been taking care of her siblings ever since she was old enough to reach the cabinets for their afternoon snack. She had been changing diapers as soon as her mom had the third kid. In this moment, Lillian felt like she could breathe and be a teenager again.

Lillian sighed, "I guess I thought I would come off as ungrateful. That's the last thing I want her to think, but being here with everyone, I feel like I can breathe. I think I can tell her that I *am* grateful for everything she does *and* I just want a break here and there to hang out with my friends. Both can be true."

Lillian looked around the circle at everyone's faces as they listened to her talk about her family. She saw all of them looking intently, Jaya's hand still on Lillian's shoulder. Lillian leaned her head onto Jaya's shoulder to rest even more.

- - -

As Lillian got her rest, Flo felt safe to open up.

"I get you, Lillian," Flo shared. "It feels like your parents want you to be someone that you don't want to be. You want to be your own person."

"Exactly," Lillian nodded. "You get it."

"My parents just..." Flo hesitated. She looked around, wondering if this new group of people would listen to her.

As her eyes fell upon Angeli, she said, "It's okay, Flo, go ahead. You said earlier that you couldn't text me back because of your parents, right?"

"Yeah, they took away my phone for the whole summer." Flo began her story.

Before Flo had arrived at the Fourth of July event, she had not been able to talk to her friends all summer.

"Mom, please!" Flo begged. "I haven't seen anyone at all this summer. You won't even let me text my friends that I'm alive and okay! It's just the Fourth of July thing at school. There's going to be so many people there."

"FLO! ¡YA!"[20] Her mom yelled. "I won't have you going out late at night, doing all types of bad stuff!"

"Dad, please. Mom is being so unreasonable. I just want to see my friends!"

"Florencia, listen to your mother," her dad reasoned.

"It's not fair at all! I don't even know why you two would think I'm doing bad things. Like, what 'bad things' could even happen?! It's a *family* event!" Flo slapped her hands on her thighs, frustrated that her parents didn't trust her.

———————————————

[20] *(Spanish)* "Enough!"

It's been one month since she's said a word to Angeli, Shiloh, or Frankie. They've been wondering why Flo had disappeared all of June, but she was just at home. She has had zero contact with anyone outside of her house and spent the last month listening to her parents try and justify their reasons for keeping her away from her phone.

"Summer is a time for you to spend time with your family. Not with friends."

"You might go out and do drugs, drink, hang out with whoever! We don't know! Stay home."

"Your friends might pressure you to do so many dangerous things out there!"

Flo never understood why her parents made these baseless assumptions. It didn't matter that she was a good student who never got in trouble at school. Her parents didn't trust her.

"Mom, Dad, please. Just for one night only and I can spend the rest of the summer at home with you guys. Please." Flo begged with her puppy dog eyes at her parents.

Her mom and dad looked at each other, then looked at Flo.

"Fine, Flo. You can go to the event." Her dad gave in to Flo's pleading eyes.

"Really?! Oh, thank you!" Flo hugged her dad.

Her mom got Flo's phone out of her dresser drawer and said, "There are conditions to you going out, Flo."

"Conditions?" Flo questioned.

"You can stay out until 9:00 p.m., but you have to text us every 30 minutes letting us know what you are doing and who you are with." Her mom handed back her phone. "And I get this phone back after you come home, okay?" Her mom waved her finger sternly.

Flo sighed, "Okay then." She grabbed her phone solemnly. She thought to herself, "EVERY 30 minutes?! That's way too much!" But couldn't risk the golden opportunity of finally getting out.

"And you better not try anything bad, Flo. We will find out, so don't even try it," her dad warned.

Flo didn't say anything back to her parents as she got ready and left the house. Even though she was glad to be going out to see her friends, she still felt like she wasn't able to relax.

After finishing her story, Flo exclaimed, "I don't know what gave them the idea I would even do anything dangerous in the first place! Like, drugs? I would never do that, *especially* after what they told me about Guatemala. I just wish they understood that I'd never do anything to hurt them or risk my safety."

"Is that where your parents are from? Guatemala? What happened there?" Sai asked

"Guatemala is very unsafe right now. It's actually why

my parents came here in the first place. There's a ton of drug trafficking, gang violence, and other really dangerous things. So, they came here to raise a family in a safe place."

Sai had a puzzled look on her face. "Hmmm," she said, "Maybe that's it, Flo? Maybe they're just scared. They've seen what things like drugs can do to people and the thought of you potentially getting wrapped up in that scares them."

Flo's eyes widened at Sai's epiphany about Flo's parents.

"I know it's frustrating, Flo," Lillian comforted her. But I think they're just trying to keep you-"

"Trying to keep me safe," Flo completed Lillian's thought. It led her to realize that it was not that her parents didn't trust *her*, they didn't trust this scary world. They've seen the evils that can come from drug use and they were just concerned for their daughter's safety. Especially now that she's getting older.

"I guess," Flo began, "I guess, I never thought of it that way. I just want them to ease up on me and trust me. Honestly, I would never do any of those things because I know how they feel about it and what they've been through," Flo's voice trembled.

Lillian replied, "I think you should tell them, Flo. I think you should tell them to try and trust you. You're not asking for much, just to text your friends over the summer!"

Flo nodded her head. She was flooded with ideas on how to talk to her parents. She knew now that her parents had her best interest in mind, but it didn't mean that they could just keep her from talking to her friends either.

Flo sniffled and wiped her eyes, "Thank you, guys." Everyone smiled softly at her in response.

- - -

Angeli stood up and laughed, "You know, it's good that you're gonna talk to them, Flo! That way we can actually talk over the summer!"

She turned away from the group and looked at the view from the hill. Angeli took a deep breath of the summer air, "I don't think I could ever talk to my parents. I never get to say *any*thing," she tucked her loose strand of hair back into her hijab.

Mark was surprised at what his sister said, "What do you mean, Angeli?"

Angeli whipped around to glare at Mark, "Of course *you* don't know! Mama and Papa *never* treat you like this! You have a later curfew and you never have to clean the house, just me!" Angeli turned to the group now to let her emotions out, "They always call me disrespectful and hard-headed. It's like I'm always punished when I don't even do anything wrong!" Angeli sat back down in the circle and started tearing the grass in frustration.

Mark, turning to Sai, loudly whispered, "Yeah, they do call her 'hard-headed' a lot, actually."

Sai rolled her eyes at Mark and turned to Angeli, "Do you think there's a reason why they're like that, Angeli?"

Angeli grunted, "It's been this way for years and it's always over little things. For example, I'm the only Muslim[21] in the family, and during Ramadan[22], they were so judgmental of me for fasting. I didn't eat at a family party, and they were *so mad* at me, practically shoving food in my face. I constantly declined and, at one point, told them they were making me feel uncomfortable. Mama told me I was rude for not eating the food and that I shouldn't have 'talked back' by saying how I felt. She kept saying 'walang hiya ka[23]' over and over and over and over!"

Angeli looked up to see the puzzled looks on everyone's faces, "*Walang hiya ka* basically means that I have no shame about my actions." She took a deep breath and sighed, "I just wish they understood that me speaking my mind doesn't make me disrespectful, even if it's to my elders."

"Maybe she was protecting you...?" Mark mumbled.

"Huh?! What do you mean *protecting me*?" Angeli

---

21 **Muslim**: A person who practices the religion of Islam.

22 **Ramadan**: The ninth month of the Muslim year, during which strict fasting is observed from sunrise to sunset.

23 *(Tagalog)*: "You have no shame."

raised an eyebrow and failed to mask her annoyance.

"I don't know, Angeli," Mark explained. "Do you remember the stories Mama would tell us about her childhood in the Philippines? She was practically your age and her elders used to pick on her a lot. They would comment on her weight, her face, her hair, her hobbies- and when she finally stood up for herself and called them out on it, she was the one who was punished. Lolo[24] used to hurt her and call her disrespectful. It just seems like that's all Mama and Papa know. Being quiet and 'respectful' kept them safe."

"So, what?" Angeli disputed. "Am I supposed to just not say anything? That doesn't help me at all, Mark." Angeli crossed her arms over her chest.

"I don't think it's that." Frankie interrupted. "I think it's amazing that you speak up for yourself, but maybe knowing *why* they say things like that might make you less angry toward them, you know? They're raising you guys the best way they can with what they know."

Angeli uncrossed her arms from her chest and rested her palms against the grass. "I mean, I never thought of it that way." Angeli lowered her gaze to the ground, "I never considered that they probably treat me this way because they don't want me to go through what they went through when they were my age. Maybe when I stand up for myself, I remind my Mama of herself when she was my age... and that scares her."

---

[24] *(Tagalog)*: Grandfather.

"Maybe next time," Mark said to Angeli, "I can be there with you so that we can talk about them treating you differently than me. I never liked it either, Angeli, it's just hard to talk to them."

Angeli looks up from the ground and at her brother. She always thought that Mark wouldn't stand up for her because he was selfish, but she now realizes it was because Mark was also afraid of their parents just as much as she was.

"I never knew you felt that way, Angeli, but I'm glad you're telling me now." Mark smiled at his sister.

Angeli smiled back at her brother, comforted by the fact that Mark was never against her.

- - -

Mark's smile began to fade. "I know you said that they treat you differently, but I have my own issues with Mama and Papa, too." He looked down at the ground and fiddled with his shoelace.

"Wait," Jaya interrupted his thoughtful gaze, "*You?* Out of all people, Mark De Los Santos has a *problem* with someone? What could your parents have against *you*? You literally have never gotten in trouble at school and you're the nicest person I know!"

Sai reiterated, "Yeah, right? Mark is always so nice to everyone. Every time he tells me something about his parents, I get so shocked because Mark couldn't even hurt a fly."

Mark suddenly stood up, surprising the group. His fists were clenched at his side and his gaze was still toward the ground. Suddenly, tears began to trickle down his cheeks and hit the grass.

"I just feel like I'm not in charge of my own life! It's either a doctor, lawyer, or *nothing*; there's no in-between. I don't *get* to be anything else! I don't *want* to go through medical school or law school!" Mark's voice was beginning to shake as the whole group turned their attention to Mark De Los Santos, in all his vulnerability. He kept it cool all the time at school, making this sudden burst of emotion catch everyone off-guard, even Angeli, his own sister.

Mark wiped his eyes and his voice quivered, "I'd rather do something with *people*. Not with books or studying. I feel way more like myself when I'm with my friends and my family, not getting A's in classes. Ever since the incident, they just don't trust me to make any decision at all."

"What incident?" Lillian asked.

Mark started telling the story of the incident that drastically changed the relationship he had with, not just his parents, but with Angeli too.

Right before summer started, Mark had started a vlog[25] titled, "Thoughts on The Hill". The vlogs were simple one- to three-minute videos of Mark sharing his various daily thoughts at the very hill that currently sat underneath the group's feet. His videos

---

[25] **Vlog**: A form of blog for which the medium is video; also known as a video blog or video log.

had gotten quite popular because Mark was naturally lovable and talked about topics that a lot of people his age would otherwise go through alone. In one vlog, he was talking about the constant pressure he felt from his mother to be a perfect son for her, even if it meant doing stuff that he didn't want to do. In particular, Mark expressed his love of connecting with others and how he hopes to incorporate that into his future career, whatever that may be. The vlog went viral because Mark was able to be authentic and vulnerable, but it had circulated to his mom. His mom was so ashamed and angry at him. She blamed social media for turning her son into someone she couldn't recognize, but in reality, it allowed Mark to be exactly who he wanted to be.

"After she saw the video, she said that I brought shame upon our family; that it was an embarrassment. She no longer trusted me, which is why she's been asking Angeli to practically babysit me and watch my every move. Even after all that, though, I still just want to be able to do what *I want* to do with my future, but I feel like I can't." Mark looked down, feeling the imposed shame that his mom instilled in him.

Sai stood alongside Mark and held his hand so he could calm down. Sai proposed, "Have you ever told your parents that you don't want to do that?"

The De Los Santos siblings looked at each other and bursted out laughing. The sudden outburst frightened the group, especially after the fact that Mark was crying not even thirty seconds ago. The De Los Santos siblings were truly peculiar.

Mark laughed, "Are you crazy? It's bad enough for Angeli to say she just needs ten more minutes before she can help out with chores, let alone, tell them I don't want to be in the medical field! They might just explode."

Benji shrugged, "Your parents sound like mine. They're more concerned about how what you do impacts the entire family instead of how it impacts just yourself. I guess it's not a *bad* thing, but it feels almost impossible to keep that up forever. You won't always be able to think about them when making every single choice. Some decisions are what's right for you alone, and that's okay."

It registered in Mark's head, "Now that you mention it, it *was* always about finding a career that makes a lot of money more than anything. It's not just about being financially stable enough to support myself, but also for me to be able to support my family if they ever need it." Mark was shocked at the words as they came out of his mouth, realizing that his parents' only wish was for Mark to not struggle as much as they had to.

He continued, "I just wish they understood that family *is* my number one priority, but I guess we just don't express it the same way. They show they care by constantly working overtime and sacrificing their time and money to make sure everyone is taken care of. But I show I care by spending time with everyone, making gifts I know they'll love, and celebrating with them during their accomplishments. We don't really hang out with friends during school breaks because we *want* to be with family, but when it gets like this, it's so overwhelming."

Frankie interjected, "I think you should say that. You should say that just because you do something different than them, it doesn't mean it's wrong. I don't think you have to choose between being your own person and caring for your family, you can do both at the same time. You can tell your parents that both of those things can be true."

Mark and Angeli looked at one another, their laughter now far subsided. They looked at each other with the hope that maybe they *could* have this difficult conversation with their parents, but also with the fear that their parents wouldn't listen. That they wouldn't understand.

Angeli asked Mark, "I don't know. I guess I'm just hesitant. Do you think they'll trust you? Us?"

Mark took a seat next to his sister and replied, "I don't know either, Angeli, but I guess that's it. I don't think we'll know until we try. We have to do it together so it's less scary." Mark grabbed his sister's hand in solidarity.

- - -

As the De Los Santos siblings had a moment of unity with each other, Sai suddenly started to cry.

"Sai? Are you okay?" Mark asked.

"It's just a lot, hearing everyone's stories. It made me think about my own stuff. I normally really don't like sharing. I actually only open up to Mark about most things, but everyone's just been so nice about hearing each other out. My parents-" Sai starts to choke up and cry into her hands.

Mark scoots over to sit closer to Sai and offer her comfort. Sai leaned onto Mark and continued, "They wouldn't even drop me off here because they were so mad at the fact that I didn't get good grades this past school year. I got a 2.23 GPA, but honestly, I was just happy I made it through the year!" Sai started to get worked up remembering that it *was* a hard year, and she should be celebrating her success, even if it wasn't up to her parents' expectations.

Sai got up from leaning on Mark and wiped her tears roughly, "So many of my uncles and cousins are in engineering, tech, or medical! Do you know what it's like to bring a 2.23 GPA home to Indian parents in a family full of smart people? It's horrible!" Sai exhaled.

"I just wish they understood that they make me feel like my value, as a person and as their daughter, depends on what grades I get. Mr. Pult, the photography teacher, was so impressed with my work that he put it on display for each of his classes. When I told my parents about it, they didn't even care and asked, "How about your math test? What grade did you get?' They don't see that the more pressure I feel from them, the *worse* my grades get."

"What do you mean?" asked Ricardo.

"The stress, the lack of sleep, the fear that I'm not going to do well. It all comes from the pressure they give me. I work so hard on studying, but when I take the tests, I panic and imagine my parents being so disappointed in me. It makes me feel like if I don't get an A, I don't deserve love." Sai laid onto Mark's shoulder again, feeling overwhelmed. She thought back to her mother's stinging words that she would repeat after every bad grade, "Mazak nahi kar rahaa hun. Agar tumne yeh dohrayaa toh acha nahi hoga."[26]

"So, let's say you do get all A's," Flo interjected, "What then? Do they think that's like, the key to happiness?"

In deep thought, Sai said, "No, I don't think that's it."

Angeli replied, "Is it like Mark's thing where, like, everything you do is for the family?"

"I mean, it may be some of that, but something else too." Sai's head turned on like a lightbulb and her face softened from crying. "If they had stayed in India and had me there, I would probably not even be able to do half of the things I get to do now. Most of my aunties and girl-cousins aren't as successful as the men in their families and it's because they couldn't get the same opportunities. India is pretty strict on gender roles."

Jaya marveled, "Yeah... yeah! That makes sense. It's like they just want you to take advantage of being here and want you to do super well since the environment here kind of allows for that. At the same time, though, it *is* a lot of pressure. Also, it doesn't explain the so-called embarrassment that led them to not want to come here today, does it?"

---

[26] *(Hindi)* "I'm not kidding. It won't be good if you repeat this."

Sai finally calmed down from her crying, "I feel like it's common in Indian culture. It's like, if something 'shameful' happens, you avoid others to experience that shame in private. It's really traditional."

Frankie mused, "Oh, so like, saving face?"

"Yes! Saving face! After they found my report card, they didn't want to come to this event. I really wanted to, though, so I begged them. Obviously, they eventually let me go, but only if I went alone without them." Sai was no longer sad about it, but more willing to talk to her parents about how she understood why they felt like A's were important, however, the pressure was affecting her mentally.

"Are you going to talk to them, Sai?" Flo asked.

"I think I just need to tell them my point of view and that the pressure is what's making me crumble. I can ask them to celebrate my wins and support me through my losses. I think I just want to know that they still love me and that they still see me as a good daughter." Sai heard herself, for the first time, say exactly what she needed to say to her parents.

"Honestly, Sai, that's perfect," Lillian says with a smile.

"It sounds like you know exactly what you need to say," Mark says as reassurance.

"Thank you, everyone. I feel so much better," Sai exhaled deeply and her shoulders relaxed for the first time in a long time.

- - -

Ricardo, on the other hand, felt Sai's emotions as his own. He started to cry again after seeing Sai's tear-stained cheeks. Sai turned to Ricardo, "Are you okay, Ricardo?"

"I'm sorry, I'm sorry." Ricardo fanned his hands toward his face to calm himself down.

Sai scoots over to Ricardo and rubs his back, "It's okay to let it out." Right when Sai said that, Ricardo started to cry even harder.

"I know it's okay to cry," he sobbed, "but my dad makes me feel like I can't." Ricardo touched his hand to his chest, "It's like, I feel *so much* shame for crying, but I can't help it. It's like I can't even, uh, even, even be a human being!" Ricardo's stammering voice echoed throughout the group, his anger beginning to overtake the sadness. Ricardo pulled out his phone and read the text that his dad sent him again, "'When you're ready to be a man' like, what does that even mean?! Why can't I be a *sensitive* man?!" He slammed his phone against the ground, the phone slightly bouncing back.

"But see what happens when you don't allow yourself to be sad? You let anger cover it up and take over." Jaya picks up his phone and hands it back to him. She gently adds, "I don't want you to stop being yourself, Ricardo."

36

Ricardo twiddles with the phone in his hands, "My dad is just... so *machismo*[27], and I don't think I'll ever be the type of man that he expects me to be. Like him."

"What's *machismo*?" asked Mark.

Lillian explained, "*Machismo* is like this idea that men have to be manly. They have to kind of be like a tough, macho man who is in charge of everything in the family. You have to be hardened, have a lot of pride, and most of the time, emotions aren't really part of being *machismo*. My dad is kind of like that and my uncles too."

"It sounds like toxic masculinity," Mark thought aloud.

Ricardo butted, "No, no, you don't get it. I mean..." Ricardo hesitated as he pieced together the possibility that his dad's version of *machismo* might also be toxic. "In Mexican culture, it's more about how the man is the provider and the protector of the family."

"But even so," Benji countered, "Why can't you show emotions? How does that change that you're a man?"

Ricardo sat with this question for a bit, twiddling the phone in his hand nervously, "I guess I just wish he understood that just because I cry easily doesn't make me any less of a man."

Lillian hugged her knees to her chest, "You're right.

---

[27] **Machismo** *(Spanish)*: The sense of being "manly" and self-reliant; behaviors associated with masculinity in the Latinx culture.

You're not less of a man just because you're sensitive. Sensitivity is a gift! You're able to feel your feelings so deeply, the good ones and the unpleasant ones. If I'm being honest, it sounds like your dad just doesn't want to see you hurt, but since he doesn't know how to say that, he comes off in a harsh way."

Ricardo stopped crying in astonishment at what Lillian said to him. Thank you, Lillian, that was so beautifully said." Ricardo started to slowly tear up again, "What should I tell him?"

Sai, still rubbing Ricardo's back, responded, "I think you could say that you feel more judged than understood. And that just because you cry or get sad doesn't mean that you're not a man. It just means that sometimes, you react to things differently than him."

"Yeah," Ricardo said, "Maybe I can help him understand my feelings a bit more. I don't want to disappoint him, I just want him to support me." Ricardo gave a slight smile to the group and turned to Sai, "Thank you for comforting me. Thank you, everyone."

"Of course. Always!" Mark exclaimed with a big smile.

- - -

After Ricardo finished, Benji felt compelled to share with the group. For once, Benji felt *seen* by this group, anticipating that they may be able to understand him. "It seems like there's a common theme going on: you guys' parents showing love in unexpected ways. My parents definitely don't make me feel loved. At all."

"What do you mean, Benji?" Ricardo asked, wiping the last of his tears.

"Well, after the school year ended, we went to Hong Kong to visit my family. The whole time I was there, not a day went by when my parents didn't compare me to my cousins. I felt like crap the whole time. They were like 'Oh, look, Zháo, so-and-so cooks dinner for *their* parents, *you* never cook dinner for us!' or like 'See, Zháo, so-and-so has *five* scholarships, YOU don't even have *one*!" There was a tone of disgust as he regurgitated his parents' words.

"Zháo?" Frankie asked.

"Yeah, 'Benji' is my English name, and 'Zháo' is my Chinese name. It's easier for friends and teachers to say 'Benji'," he explained.

"I think Zháo is a cooler name, actually." Frankie bemused.

Benji laughed at Frankie's sudden acceptance of his Chinese name, "Thanks, man."

He continued, "When we got back here, I tried to talk to them about it. I told them 'Am *I* so-and-so? No! I'm *your son*! I'm *Zháo*! It's like I am not good enough for you!' and then they said, 'You're good, but you can be *better*.' I couldn't even believe they said that. I even told them how much that hurt me. Guess what they did after I told them that." Benji gestured to the group.

"...Apologize?" Jaya guessed.

Benji made a low, bellowed laugh, "Nothing! They didn't do anything! Not even a 'sorry' from them. They're pretending like it never happened. They don't ever hug me or tell me that they love me or even apologize." Benji's tone softened, "I just wish they understood that it hurts to see my friends get hugged by their parents over every little thing they succeed at, and I don't get to experience the same. Later that day, my mom came into my room to tell me to go downstairs because she cooked *Xiao Long Bao*[28], which is my favorite food. But she was still totally ignoring that we got into that huge fight."

Angeli starts laughing, "Oh my goodness! My mom does that too! She never says 'sorry', but she comes into my room with sliced fruit after an argument."

Benji's eyes widened, "No way? She does that too?"

Sai laughed as well, "Yeah, my mom too. She'll cook my favorite food whenever we butt heads. I think it's their way of apologizing."

Benji wondered, "I guess you're right. It's so simple!" Benji's hands moved expressively with realization, "I guess my mom says 'I love you' or 'I'm sorry' through food. Now that I think about it, they *do* express more through actions than through words... Maybe I took the comparison wrong? Maybe they were just trying to push me to be the best version of myself and to never

---

[28] **Xiao Long Bao**: A type of small Chinese steamed bun, traditionally served in a bamboo steaming basket.

settle."

Angeli retorted, "Even so, it's okay for you to ask them for a bit of verbal validation, too, you know?"

Benji smiled at Angeli, "That's also true. It's not really common in traditional Chinese culture to say that you love each other. It's more common to do it through actions."

Frankie added, "I know you said you already tried to talk to them, but sometimes we need to tell people things more than once for them to understand how important it is to us. I think you should try and talk to them again about it since it's still bothering you. Don't let it fester."

"Maybe this time, I could let them know that I see that they love me through their actions, but that it would be helpful to hear them tell me they're proud of who I am right *now*," Benji concluded.

Suddenly, Shiloh, who had been quiet the duration of their time on the hill, said, "I think that would help a lot, Benji."

- - -

Everyone turned to Shiloh, shocked that they started to talk. The group had an expectation that Shiloh was going to be a silent supporter, especially after Mark accidentally misgendered them. Frankie saw Shiloh slightly revert into themself due to the sudden interjection of their voice shaking the group.

Frankie then lightly nudged Shiloh, "Want to tell them what you were telling me and Flo earlier?"

Shiloh sits up straighter as they prepare themself to talk, "I wasn't going to share. But everyone's been so nice to one another that it inspired me to share my own stuff too."

They took a deep breath, "I'm sure I'm seen as the quiet person who is not really friends with anyone. To tell you the truth, it hasn't always been that way. I want to say it started around middle school when everyone began to split into groups and cliques, finding what they liked and didn't like. I felt like such an outcast most of the time and the thought of coming to school made me feel sick. I just felt so empty and alone and I really wasn't sure why."

Shiloh closed their eyes, as if remembering a painful memory, "When I talked to my parents, they told me to stop being dramatic. They told me to just 'suck it up', or that I had to just get through the week, or that things will get better as I get older. It was just so unbearable. It felt like I couldn't be myself because I didn't even know who I was. I felt so lost. Because I felt that way, I really didn't want to be here anymore." Shiloh's voice quivered after they uttered the word "anymore".

"I would see some of you hang out with each other and I wanted that so bad. Most days, I spent my time at the library and, one day, I stumbled across some book about Pride."

"Oh! I think I know what you're talking about! It's

like, the only book about the LGBTQ+ community in there, but I guess it's a start." Benji pressed his lips together in slight annoyance and shrugged.

"I know, right? Ugh! But you're right. It is a start. At the time, I didn't really see it as that. It was more like finding a beacon of light and, at the time, I never even knew about being trans or being non-binary. But when I read about it," Shiloh crossed their hands over their heart, "I felt so seen. I finally felt understood. It felt like I was finally able to fill in the gap that made me feel lonely and excluded all those years. It finally put words to my experiences. I even learned about the *muxe*[29] people of Oaxaca! It felt so special to me."

"Do your parents know?" asked Jaya.

"I mean, they do know. They're kind of floating around it. I asked them if I could go to therapy or talk to a professional, just so I could discover and learn more about myself. But like I said earlier," Shiloh motioned to Frankie and Flo, recalling where they left off in their earlier conversation, "My parents are not really helping me figure that out. It's like they're brushing it off as if my feelings aren't real enough to take seriously. I mean, I get that they had 'real' problems. Like when they immigrated here from Oaxaca, they had to focus on survival, finding food, and getting shelter. Compared to that, *my* stuff is more... I guess... invisible," their voice trailed, "I just wish they understood that just because you can't *see* my feelings, and my problems look different than

---

[29] **Muxe** *(myū-heh):* The third gender in the Zapotec culture of Oaxaca. Someone assigned male at birth who dresses and behaves in ways otherwise associated with women.

theirs, doesn't mean they don't affect me deeply."

Jaya started to quietly tear up for her new friend, "Oh, Shiloh, I'm so sorry they don't support you as fully as you need them to. I love that you want to talk to someone about it because it's important to! Why don't they want to support you in that way?"

"I don't know. My parents came from Oaxaca right before I was born. So, like a lot of you mentioned, immigrating was really hard on them. I figured it was because *they* never got therapy or counseling for their own stuff, so they figured that I didn't need it. But, the difference is, my parents have each other, but I don't have anyone who I could relate to. Since they don't want to deal with it, it makes *me* not want to deal with it either.

Flo added, "That makes a lot of sense though, Shiloh. It's not that your problems are shameful or embarrassing or not-real. I guess it's because they don't know what might be the best way to support you since they're not really familiar with talking to a therapist."

"You're right, Flo," Shiloh replied, "I guess they think that solving problems is a one-size-fits-all type of deal. I mean, the book really helped me discover things about my identity, but I still have *so many* questions, especially about mental health and stuff. I was so deeply unhappy before I started learning who I am, I don't ever want it to get that bad again."

"Have you thought about going to the school counselor? Mrs. Diaz?" Jaya asked.

"... We have a school counselor??" Shiloh exclaimed, their eyes wide.

Jaya laughed, "Yeah! She's so helpful. She helped me a lot with my stuff and it's confidential! I go to her about once a month, sometimes weekly if I need to. She could help you find resources about exploring your identity and support you in taking care of your mental health!"

"That's the thing," Shiloh said, "I don't want to keep this from my parents. We don't ever lie to one another or keep secrets."

"Are you going to talk to them about it?" Mark asked.

"I'd really like to. I love my parents and I know that they just want me to be okay. But my mental health is important and I want them- actually, *need* them to be a part of the journey. So, I think I could start with the school counselor."

Angeli asked, "How do you think you'll bring it up?"

"Maybe I can tell them that seeing a counselor is something I want to do. I can tell them that it would be great if I could share with them everything that I learn and give them the chance to understand me more too. I just want to be as strong as them. I admire them so much. I just need some additional help, and now I'm learning that that's okay." Shiloh smiled warmly at the group, thanking them silently for their attention to them as they shared their experience.

- - -

As the sun began to set below the horizon, the group felt lighter from their talk with one another. It was about 15 minutes before the fireworks would start, indicating that it was time for the group to go back down to the main field. They all started to stand up and collect themselves.

Sai asked Flo to check if it was obvious that she had been crying, to which Flo said, "Not at all," as she wiped the last of the tears from Sai's face. As Mark rose, he went over to Angeli to help her up from the ground. They hugged each other and started laughing at the grass that stuck to Mark's jeans. Lillian ran a hand through her hair as she took one last look at the view from the top of the hill, wondering if she would ever bring her siblings up here once they were older.

Ricardo joined Lillian, walking with her once they said their silent goodbyes to this safe space. Benji offered to assist Frankie down the hill with his wheelchair, to which Frankie smiled. Following close behind, Shiloh and Jaya exchanged numbers, hoping to talk with one another even more.

"I don't know about y'all," Mark started, "But I definitely feel a lot better after all of that." Mark put his arm around Angeli's shoulder.

"Haha, yeah, I feel like I vented so much. I feel like a new person, almost lighter? It feels really good," Sai added, walking with her arm linked with Flo's.

"Hey," Shiloh said from the back of the line. The group turned around to see Shiloh standing there and smiling. It was such a drastic shift from how Shiloh was when they first met with the group. "I'm really glad we all got to talk to each other."

Jaya linked her arm to Shiloh's. One by one, they made their way down into the main field. As the ground leveled, Benji looked back to see the trail up to the hill one last time. He raised his hand up toward the hill as if waving goodbye to a friend he would see again soon; thanking the hill for being a place of comfort and safety for himself and his new friends.

Part Three
Connected

As the group made their way down to the football field, they saw it was busier than earlier as families, friends, and loved ones had gathered to watch the fireworks. Mark's phone started ringing with the name "Mama" flashing across the screen.

"Hello, Ma?" Mark started.

"Hoy! Nasaan kayo?[30] Your dad and I walked around the whole football field twice and we didn't see you two!" Mark's mom yelled through the phone.

---

[30] *(Tagalog)* "Hey! Where are you?"

Putting it on speaker, Mark motioned to Angeli to say something to their mom, "Don't worry, Ma. Mark and I are together. We're on our way, we'll see you soon." Angeli paused for a second before she said, "I love you, Ma."

"Mark yelled into the phone enthusiastically, "We love you, Ma! We're coming now. Can we talk later when we get home?"

The De Los Santos siblings were the first to bid goodbye to the rest of the group. Angeli quickly hugged everyone, hoping that she'd be able to see her friends at least one more time before the summer ended.

"I think I'm going to buy some food, so I'll catch you guys later?" Sai smiled.

"For sure, Sai! If you want, you can watch the fireworks with us. I'll text you where we end up." Flo waved her phone at Sai.

Sai stood in line to buy a warm, baked potato from Juliet's Roasted Potatoes and Corn stand when she got a text from Flo, which said, "We're headed to the goalpost on the home side, meet us there c:". Sai smiled at Flo's little smiley face, grateful that she made new friends today. She continued on her phone to pass the waiting time and, as she scrolled through her contacts, she decided to call her parents.

"Hi, mom."

"Sai? Are you okay?! Why are you calling?"

"I'm okay! I'm okay! I'm just calling to check in with you before the fireworks start."

"I was talking to some friends, and I think that it might be a good idea for me to get some tutoring this summer to help with my grades a bit" Sai was listening intently to what her mom would reply with.

"Oh! Oh... Oh, okay. Yeah, why not? That's good, Sai. Does the school offer any?"

"Yeah, the school offers some. I hope it'll make you feel proud of me." Sai whispered into the phone.

"Oh, Sai, we're always proud of you," Sai's mom earnestly said. She wondered why her daughter would ever think otherwise.

"Okay, mom. I love you, maybe when I come home, we can talk for a bit?" Sai waited for her reply.

"Okay, Sai. I'll see you soon." Her mom hung up, not wanting Sai to hear her sudden tears.

Sai put her phone back into her pocket and grabbed her well-deserved baked potato. She turned to walk toward the home goalpost.

In the middle of the football field, Lillian was scanning the crowd for her family. Her eyes landed on her mom talking to a neighboring family who looked to be making simple conversation with her, "Hi! We love your picnic blanket. It's so nice!" They pointed at the intricate pattern on the blanket that Lillian's grandma gave to them right before they left. She found her mom smiling politely and looking around awkwardly, the language barrier stifling the possibility of connection.

Lillian ran to them and happily translated what the neighbors were saying. As they wished them well, Lillian's mom began chattering away at where she had been. Her siblings jumped up and ran to her to hug her around her legs. Looking around her chaotic family, Lillian smiled and said, "Mucho gusto a verlos. ¿Podémos habar cuando llegamos a la casa?"[31]

Her mom looked at her with confusion, but quickly nodded and smiled. She was just very grateful that her daughter was back with them, safe and sound.

Benji found his parents easily, as they liked to stay away from the crowd. Benji's parents sat with lawn chairs right by the parking lot. As he approached them, he saw that his mom was looking a bit cold. He picked up the blanket sticking out of their picnic bag and wrapped it around his mom's shoulders. Benji's mom was startled but relaxed when she saw it was her son, "Thank you, Zháo. Where were you?"

"Oh, just with some friends. I was thinking about getting some kettle corn before the fireworks start. Do you guys want any?" Benji put his hands on his knees to bend down toward his parents.

"Okay, Zháo." His dad smiled, "Kettle corn sounds really good right now!"

---

[31] *(Spanish)* "I'm so happy to see you. Can we talk when we get home?"

Benji got up to walk towards the kettle corn stand
when he turned around and said, "By the way, when
we get home, can we talk about something?"

Benji's parents looked at one another in wonder, but
they turned to their son and nodded with a calm look
on their faces. Benji responded with a warm smile as
he turned around to get some kettle corn.

Flo, Frankie, and Ricardo passed by Benji and his
family, waving enthusiastically. Flo heard Benji ask
his parents to talk later and gave him a comforting
thumbs up in support. Inspired by this, Flo decided to
call her mom.

"Hi, Mom."

"What's wrong? Who are you with? What are you
doing?" Flo smiled at her mom, worrying already.

"Yes, I'm okay. I just saw Angeli and some other kids
from school."

"Where are you? You know we told you to stay on the
football field."

"Mom, I'm with the crowd right now, don't worry!"
Flo took a deep breath, "Actually, I can't wait to come
home. If it's okay with you and Dad, can we talk
later?"

Flo's mom took a pause, wondering what Flo could
possibly want to talk about. All she hoped was that Flo
was all right, "Okay, Flo. We'll see you when you're
home.

Flo said bye to her mom and hung up the phone.

Ricardo, watching Flo ask her parents to talk, decided to finally text his dad back. Feeling the tinge of tears coming as he read his dad's words again, he let himself cry instead of feeling ashamed for being who he is. He texted his dad, "Hey Dad, I wish you didn't leave because I wanted to watch the fireworks with you. I get it. But I hope we can talk when you pick me up later." Ricardo anxiously shoved his phone into his pockets. Not knowing what to do and feeling himself panic, his helplessness was interrupted by Flo pulling him into a tight hug. Frankie put his hand on Ricardo's back to comfort him. As his friends surrounded him with warmth, Ricardo no longer felt the need to hide himself and let his tears fall down Flo's shoulder.

Closer to the school's main grounds, Jaya and Shiloh were busily walking through the crowd.

"I think the counselor is actually here, Shiloh! I saw her walking around earlier." Jaya was holding onto Shiloh's hand, moving them through the crowd.

Shiloh was following Jaya hurriedly as they stopped in front of Mrs. Diaz, who was waiting for the fireworks to start with her partner. She saw Jaya and smiled. She loved working with Jaya last semester. Watching Jaya understand herself more and more with each session was a special thing to witness. She noticed Shiloh, a quiet kid that she'd seen sitting alone at lunch. She always wanted Shiloh to come to counseling but believed that students needed to be ready in order to receive help from someone like her.

"Mrs. Diaz!" Jaya called out excitedly.

"Hi Jaya! How are you?" She got up and hugged Jaya tightly.

"I'm really good! I actually came over to introduce you to Shiloh. They're a new friend of mine."

"Hi, it's nice to meet you." Shiloh extended their hand to shake Mrs. Diaz's.

Mrs. Diaz mentally noted that Shiloh's pronouns are they/them and shook their hand. "It's nice to meet you, too! Are you both here with your families?" Mrs. Diaz asked.

"Actually, we're going to watch the fireworks with some new friends we made earlier. I brought Shiloh to you because they were looking to start counseling with you." Jaya's inflection lingered like a question more than a comment.

Mrs. Diaz smiled, "Of course, Shiloh. I just need a permission slip from your parents so that they're aware you're going. It's on the school website. I'm looking forward to talking with you!"

"Thank you so much." Shiloh smiled widely, excited to start this new journey.

They both said their goodbyes to Mrs. Diaz and, as they walked away, Shiloh called their dad. "Hi Dad, is Mom there? I actually have something important to tell you guys. Let's talk when I get home."

Shiloh's dad just said a neutral, "Okay. See you soon." Right before the call ended, Shiloh overheard their dad calling out to their mom, "Shiloh just called, they said they wanna talk later!" Shiloh smiled slightly hearing their dad use their correct pronouns. As the call ended, their dad questioned what could have happened to Shiloh, but most of all hoped that they were okay.

As the sun sank beyond the horizon, the fireworks suddenly lit up the sky. Everyone looked up as the cascading red, white, and blue colors of the sparks fluttered above them. The booming sound of the fireworks vibrated within everyone's chest as the sequence of explosions got bigger and more colorful. Even at different parts of the field, each of them still felt that silent comfort and safety that they felt on the hill. Putting their hands to their chest, they felt a sense of comfort burst within. The explosions in the sky were mirroring the spark of a new beginning; a new hope, a new peace.

Post-Reading Discussion

This book was the product of my clinical dissertation entitled *Creating a Book Intervention for Second-Generation Asian and Latinx Adolescents, Targeting the Parent-Child Acculturation Gap*, which I wrote for my doctoral degree in Clinical Psychology. When completing the research, I found studies that supported that bibliotherapeutic interventions (such as this book) are most effective when you think about, talk about, or act on things you've learned from the story- which is what this whole back section is for!

The inspiration for creating this book came from my personal experience as a second-generation adolescent, as well as the lived experiences of many others. Many second-generation adolescents struggle to balance their home culture with the culture of the country they live in. This can lead to confusion and misunderstandings, causing people to feel like something is wrong with themselves or their parents/family. Understandably, cultural differences can create tension. However, it's important to recognize that this does not necessarily indicate flaws in individuals or families, but rather a clash in cultures. I hope this book helps shed light on this.

This book is for the kids who were embarrassed to bring their parents' cooking to school for fear it would be "too stinky", for the kids who had to tell their friends to take their shoes off in the house and say "hi" to their parents when they'd come over, for the kids who felt like they had to live a double life, and for the kids who felt like they could never be fully understood.

The activities and discussions ahead are designed to be done between the child and caregiver(s). This might feel uncomfortable at first, it might feel awkward, it might feel daunting, and sometimes it might feel impossible. I want you to approach them with an open mind. They are **not** designed to solve problems, but they **are** built to help you (and your caregiver) open your perspectives to one another's worldview. I invite you to be curious instead of critical, be nonjudgmental instead of invalidating, and be mindful instead of reactive. One last thing to keep in mind:

nothing changes if nothing changes :-)

Some Definitions Before We Start

There's going to be a lot of words being thrown around, so let's define them first! :-)

Immigrant: A person who was born in one country, and then moved to another country to live permanently. Also known to be "first-generation".

Second-generation: A person whose parents immigrated from another country, but was born in the host country.

Host culture: The culture of the country one resides in; the dominant culture in a particular location.

Heritage culture: The culture of the country one's ethnic background.

The term **parent** and **caregiver** will be used interchangeably. **Parent** refers to someone who has given birth to an offspring while **caregiver** refers to someone who takes responsibility for the care of an offspring, despite birth status.

Worldview: How our upbringing, immediate environment, relationships, and greater society shape our values, beliefs, expectations, and morals.

Our Characters

All the characters in our story are **second-generation** adolescents. Each character faced some level of conflict around how their **worldview** and their parents' worldview clash.

Mark De Los Santos is *Filipino* and faced conflict around his personal interests versus familial interests as well as the importance of a social life.

Angeli De Los Santos is *Filipina* and faced conflict around expressing her opinions and respecting her elders.

Sai Singh is *Indian* and faced conflict around academic expectations and avoiding shame.

Zháo "Benji" Liang is *Chinese* and faced conflict around showing love and parents comparing children to others.

Lillian Vasquez is *Puerto Rican* and faced conflict around responsibilities regarding siblings and being the caregivers' language/cultural broker.

Shiloh Santiago is *Oaxacan* and faced conflict around reluctance to address mental/emotional hardships.

Ricardo De León is *Mexican* and faced conflict around disagreements on gender role expectations.

Florencia "Flo" Bautista is *Guatemalan* and faced conflict around exposure to potential dangers like substance use.

Book Club

After you and your parent(s) read this book (individually or together), ask each other the following questions to facilitate deeper conversations. The more detailed your answers, the more you can learn about one another!

1. Which character do you identify with the most? Why?
2. Which character do you identify with the least? Why?
3. What part of the story brought up the most emotion for you?
4. What did you feel was realistic and unrealistic in the story?
5. Have we ever had any conflicts or arguments like the ones in the story?
6. With *our* relationship in mind, finish this sentence: "I just wish you understood that..."
7. If you were on the hill with the characters, what story would you share about me?
8. Can the characters' conflicts with their parents be solved after *one* conversation?
9. What do you think gets in the way of conflict getting solved?
10. Like the characters in the book, do you think *we* have moments of cultural clashing? In which areas is it most apparent? How does it play out for us?
11. Is there any way you see your behaviors changing now that you've read this book?
12. What are some things you've learned from the story, either about yourself, our relationship, or in general?

Drawing Activities

If you and/or your caregiver(s) favor artistic expression over verbal expression, these activities are for you! Here are some different prompts you can use as inspiration:

Each of you draw a picture of...

- You and your family before and after reading this book
- You and your family before and after addressing something difficult
- You and your family today and 10 years from now
- You and your family 10 years ago and today.
- What your relationship looks like now and what you would like for it to look like.
- An outline of yourself and an outline of your parent(s). Draw/write things that describe their mind and heart inside the outline. Outside of the outline, draw/write how others typically see them.
- A "safe space" and share the meaning with one another. Describe what is in the "safe space" and what is not allowed.
- The images that come to mind when you think of one another. Describe and share why these images come to mind.
- Your idea of "the perfect day." Share the parts that make it perfect (activities, people involved, etc.)
- Your role model. Who are they and what is it about them that inspires you?
- Your dream home. Where is it, who lives in it, and what are the functions of each room?

Some "Get To Know You" Questions

Here are some questions you and your caregiver(s) can ask one another. As a reminder: be patient with one another. Don't just hear them talk, *listen* to what they're saying in a curious and nonjudgmental way. Observe where your answers are similar and where they differ.

1. Can you share something with me that I haven't learned about you yet?
2. What was the best part of your childhood? What was the most challenging part?
3. What is something I do that confuses you?
4. What do you like to share with others when talking about me? What makes you excited to tell them?
5. What are some things you have seen your parents do that you want to continue as a parent? What are some things you wish to discontinue?
6. What would you say has been the biggest obstacle in our relationship? How do *you* think we can solve this?
7. What has been the funniest moment in our relationship?
8. How would you define love?
9. How would you describe the perfect parent-child relationship?
10. What would you say is *my* greatest accomplishment? What would you say is *your* greatest accomplishment?
11. What are some things you agree/disagree with within our **heritage culture**?
12. What are some things you agree/disagree with within our **host culture**?

Expressing & Receiving Love

Based on how our parents/caregivers treated us, the environment we grew up in, the media we were exposed to, the friends we've surrounded ourselves with, the greater society, and so many other innumerable factors, our idea of how we express love and receive love can vary between people. Some different ways people have categorized how they best express/ receive love include gifts, spending quality time, performing acts of service, exchanging physical touch, and expressing words of affirmation.

Sometimes, how we express love and how we receive love may not match. Take some time with your parent(s) to understand how you both can communicate love to one another in a way that the other will best appreciate. Include specific behaviors and examples.

	Expressing Love	Receiving Love
My Preference		
Their Preference		

Let's Talk Conflict

Think back to the last time there was a parent-child conflict in your relationship. What was it about? What emotions came up? It can be difficult to recall painful memories *and* it can be helpful to process exactly what happened and how it happened to move forward in a way that helps us to heal. What informs us of what is right and wrong is our **worldview**. Immigrant parents and their second-generation offspring are bound to have some conflicting worldviews given the stark difference in their experiences.

Let's break down some past conflicts with this nifty little chart! Feel free to either use this page or fold a separate piece of paper into four equal squares with the headers listed in our example. Allow both you and your parent(s) to complete this chart as objectively and non-judgmentally as possible, compare your answers, and discuss the similarities/differences.

	What is the *real* problem?	How can it be solved?
My Perspective		
Their Perspective		

Our Timeline

It's important to remember that our parent(s) have a whole life story that existed before we came into the picture. As we navigate through life's milestones, we may find that our paths cross with theirs in meaningful and surprising ways.

With you and your parent(s), cut a sheet of paper into 3 long and even strips (but still large enough to write on). Tape the strips end-to-end so that they become one super-long strip. Repeat this process as many times as necessary.

Turn the super-long strip over (on the side with no tape), and draw a straight line down the middle all the way to the end. On this timeline, mark important dates and events in chronological order. Each family member should use different colors to differentiate experiences. Mark the different years across the timeline, even better if you could include dates for each of the events! Here are some ideas of things to mark on your timeline:

- Birthdays
- Significant deaths
- Moves
- Starting or ending a job
- Competitions
- Family arguments

- Periods of hardship
- Pivotal interactions
- Celebrations and accomplishments
- Memories that stand out to you (no matter how small)

Once you all have completed the timeline, discuss any observations you have, overlapping experiences, or anything new you've learned about one another. Ask each other questions about experiences on the timeline and listen non-judgmentally to how it impacted them.

FINAL NOTE TO THE READER

Thank you for indulging in *Can We Talk? A Short Story of Navigating Identity and Belonging as Teens of Immigrant Parents*. I hope this book was helpful, validating, refreshing, perspective-shifting, and healing. For more information about this book or the team, please visit:

www.instagram.com/canwetalk.book/